This book belongs to:

_____

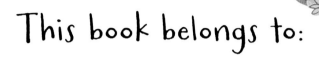

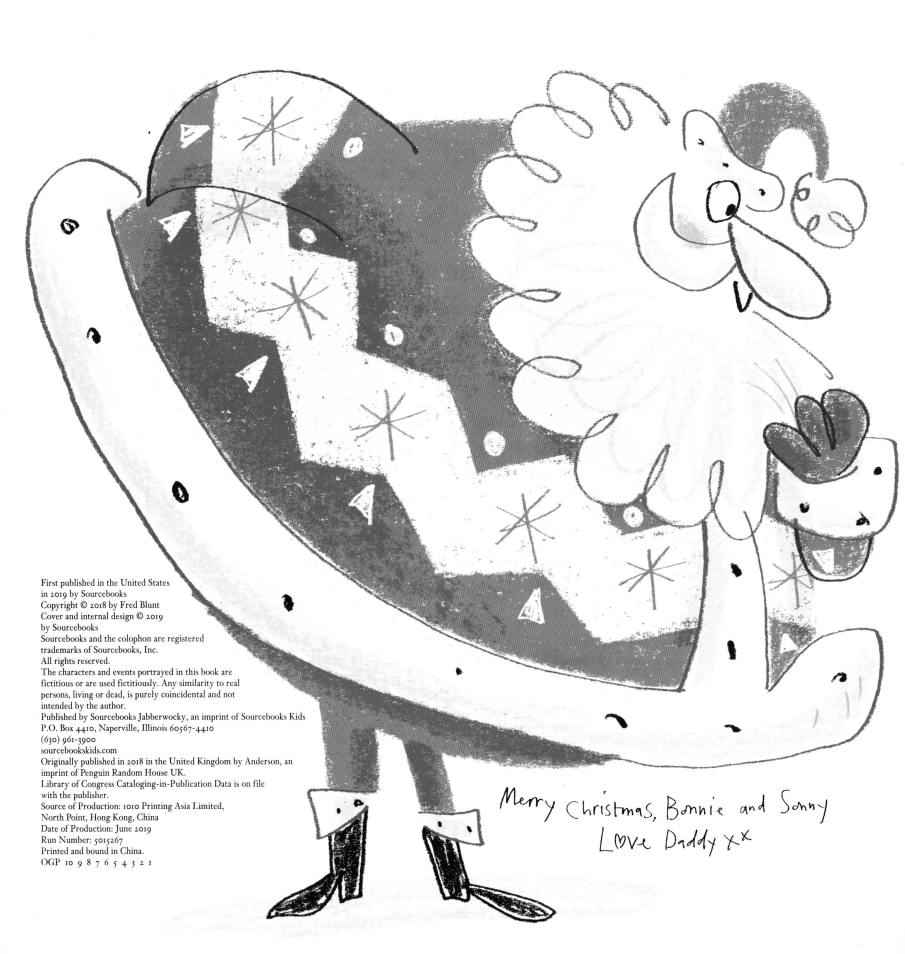

First published in the United States
in 2019 by Sourcebooks
Copyright © 2018 by Fred Blunt
Cover and internal design © 2019
by Sourcebooks
Sourcebooks and the colophon are registered
trademarks of Sourcebooks, Inc.
All rights reserved.
The characters and events portrayed in this book are
fictitious or are used fictitiously. Any similarity to real
persons, living or dead, is purely coincidental and not
intended by the author.
Published by Sourcebooks Jabberwocky, an imprint of Sourcebooks Kids
P.O. Box 4410, Naperville, Illinois 60567-4410
(630) 961-3900
sourcebookskids.com
Originally published in 2018 in the United Kingdom by Anderson, an
imprint of Penguin Random House UK.
Library of Congress Cataloging-in-Publication Data is on file
with the publisher.
Source of Production: 1010 Printing Asia Limited,
North Point, Hong Kong, China
Date of Production: June 2019
Run Number: 5015267
Printed and bound in China.
OGP 10 9 8 7 6 5 4 3 2 1

Merry Christmas, Bonnie and Sonny
Love Daddy xx

SANTA CLAUS Vs THE EASTER BUNNY

Fred BLunT

sourcebooks
jabberwocky

Santa Claus and the Easter Bunny
lived next door to each other.
Santa was a jolly fellow.
Bunny was not.

You see, down in his garden workshop, Bunny first had to make the chocolate...

then turn the chocolate into eggs...

then wrap them
(even though the foil put his teeth on edge)...

all before delivering them
all by himself.

(Which explains why you often
find Easter eggs scattered
all over your yard.)

Bunny didn't have
a shiny factory or
a team of elves.

Keep it up,
elves! Only
two million
toys to go.

Nor did Bunny have a herd of magic, flying reindeer to help him on his delivery route.

And for all his hard work, Bunny
never received a single thank-you—

unlike Santa, who
gets tasty treats
from children all
over the world.

Milk and cookies in America

Coffee in Sweden

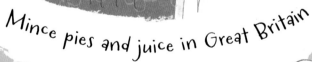
Mince pies and juice in Great Britain

Rice pudding in Denmark

And... thank-you letters from
the kind children of Germany

Determined to get even with Santa
and those ungrateful children,
Bunny decided to hatch a plan.

He thought...

and thought...

and thought harder still...

until a deliciously
devious plot popped
into his head!

HOT
CHOC

Later that night, the Easter Bunny snuck over to Santa's workshop.

He climbed down the giant chimney, just like Santa himself, then tiptoed past the silent conveyor belts.

When he got to the merry manufacturing machines,
he pumped them full of warm liquid chocolate.

On Christmas Eve, it was business as usual in Santa's workshop. Almost finished for the year, the tired elves never noticed that the toys were being made with chocolate.

That night, Bunny went to bed early, imagining
Santa racing around the world...

And the sad faces of disappointed
children as their toys melted
into blobs of chocolate!

On Christmas morning,
Bunny kicked off
his blankets, raced
downstairs,

hopped into his
favorite chair,

and turned on
the television.

Bunny couldn't believe it.
Santa was more popular than ever.

THAT'S IT. I QUIT. NO MORE EASTER BUNNY. NO MORE EGGS. SANTA CAN DO IT ALL FROM NOW ON. AT LEAST HE'LL BE THANKED. SNIFF.

With a heavy heart, Bunny decided to close his workshop and leave town for good.

He was just saying goodbye to his cozy little house when the doorbell rang...

It was Santa!

Bunny didn't like the sound of that.

Before long, Santa had built a state-of-the-art workshop, including a chocolate fountain for the sweet-toothed elves.

CHOCLONATOR 2000

Bunny was a happy bunny indeed.
And as for Santa, well, he was always happy.

The End.